Stormy's Hat

Just Right for a Railroad Man

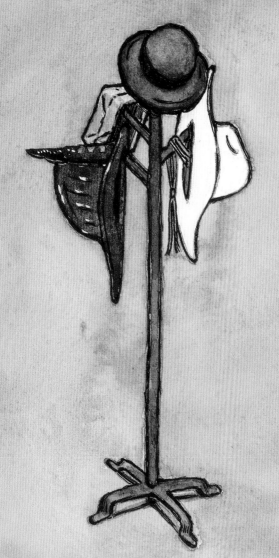

Eric A. Kimmel • Pictures by Andrea U'Ren

FARRAR, STRAUS AND GIROUX / NEW YORK

To Howard Wallace, conductor, and Elvin Wallace,
engineer, on the New York Central Railroad
—E.A.K.

For Beverly Reingold, Robbin Gourley, Lisa Graff,
and Margaret Ferguson—for their unparalleled support and patience
—A.U.

Text copyright © 2008 by Shearwater Books
Pictures copyright © 2008 by Andrea U'Ren
Distributed in Canada by Douglas & McIntyre Ltd.
Color separations by Embassy Graphics
Printed and bound in the United States of America by Phoenix Color Corporation
Designed by Jay Colvin
First edition, 2008
10 9 8 7 6 5 4 3 2 1

www.fsgkidsbooks.com

Library of Congress Cataloging-in-Publication Data
Kimmel, Eric A.
    Stormy's hat : just right for a railroad man / Eric A. Kimmel ; pictures by
Andrea U'Ren.— 1st ed.
        p.   cm.
    Summary: As Stormy, a railroad engineer, searches for the perfect hat—one
that will not blow off, get too hot, or shade his eyes too much—his wife, Ida,
becomes increasingly annoyed that he will not let her help. Includes a historical
note about the real Stormy and Ida Kromer.
    ISBN-13: 978-0-374-37262-0
    ISBN-10: 0-374-37262-4
    [1. Hats—Fiction.   2. Railroads—Trains—Fiction.   3. Sewing—Fiction.]
    I. U'Ren, Andrea, ill.   II. Title.

PZ7.K5648 Sto 2008
[Fic]—dc22
                                                            2005051233

Stormy Kromer was an engineer. He drove a locomotive on the Red Stack line from St. Paul to Chicago. Stormy loved driving trains.

He loved the *WHOOO! WHOOO!* of the steam whistle.
He loved the *chug-chug* of the locomotive.
He loved the *poketa-poketa* sound of steel wheels rolling along
the track.

There was only one thing about his job that Stormy didn't love. He couldn't find a hat that was right for a railroad man.

One Monday morning Stormy climbed into the cab of his engine. He wore his new derby hat. As his locomotive entered the Winston Tunnel, the wind snatched that derby from his head. Stormy tried to catch it, but his hat was gone.

"Great Casey Jones!" Stormy shouted.

He complained to his wife, Ida. "That's the third hat I've lost this month. Why can't I find a hat that will stay on my head? Why can't I find a hat that's right for a railroad man?"

"Well, I've been thinking about that," said Ida. "It seems to me—"

"Aw, don't you worry your pretty little head," said Stormy. "I'll figure out something."

"A cowboy hat. That's what you need," Stormy's friend Tex told him. "Get one with bonnet strings that tie under your chin. Then your hat won't blow away."

Stormy got himself a tall, wide Stetson hat. He tied the bonnet strings under his chin, just as Tex said to do.

The hat didn't blow off in the wind, but it was so tall and wide that it kept getting in the way. The brim flopped down into Stormy's eyes when he tried to read the gauges. Oil and coal dust stained the crown. Stormy began the run with a white hat. He ended it with a black one.

"This hat might work for a cowboy, but not for me," Stormy grumbled to Ida when he got home. "I need a hat that's right for a railroad man."

"I think you should—"

"Aw, don't you worry your pretty little head," said Stormy. "I'll figure out something."

"A pressman's hat is what you need," Stormy's friend Nate suggested. Nate was a printer who ran the presses that printed the great Chicago newspapers. He showed Stormy how to fold a pressman's hat from a sheet of newspaper. "It's small, so it won't get in your way. And if it blows off or gets dirty, you just make yourself another one."

"This is the hat for me!" said Stormy. He walked down to the rail
yard wearing his new pressman's hat.

15

The hat worked out fine—until a spark from the firebox landed on it. Stormy's paper hat began to smolder. It burst into flame.

"I'm on fire!" Stormy yelled. He flung the pressman's hat out the window. Just in time!

"A pressman's hat may work for a printer, but not for me." Stormy groaned as Ida rubbed ointment on his singed scalp. "I need a hat that's right for a railroad man."

"Have you considered—"

"Aw, don't you worry your pretty little head," said Stormy. "I'll figure out something."

"Try a fireman's hat," said Stormy's friend Mike, the fireman. "My hat's made of leather, so it won't burn. If it gets dirty, just wipe it clean. The brim is in the back, so it won't get in your way. And it's heavy, so the wind won't blow it off."

"That might work!" said Stormy.

It did, for a while. The fireman's hat didn't blow off when Stormy leaned out the window. It didn't get in Stormy's way when he checked the gauges. To clean it, he just wiped it with his handkerchief. And no matter how many sparks landed on the hat, it didn't catch fire.

19

But a fireman's hat is mighty heavy and hot to wear. It gave Stormy a headache.

"My head feels like John Henry is pounding it with a sledgehammer," Stormy said to Ida as she brought him some headache tablets and a glass of water. "Policemen have hats. Sailors have hats. Even coal miners have hats! Why can't I find a hat for a railroad man?"

"Maybe if you—"

"Aw, don't you worry your pretty little head," said Stormy. "I'll figure out something."

"Well, I may not be here when you do! If you say that one more time, Stormy, I'll walk out the door and not come back. My head isn't little. It's as big as yours and just as smart. Either listen to what I have to say, or stop complaining."

"Golly!" Stormy said. "I didn't mean to hurt your feelings, Ida. I'm sorry. What do you want me to do?"

"Just talk to me the way you talk to all your friends."

Ida picked up her sketch pad and took out her drawing pencil. "I have an idea," she said. "Close your eyes and imagine you're in a hat store. You just found the perfect hat for a railroad man. What does it look like?"

Stormy leaned back in his chair and shut his eyes tight. "It has a wide brim to keep the sun out of my eyes."

Ida began to sketch.

"But not so wide that it gets in my way."

Ida erased.

"It fits tight, so it doesn't blow off in the wind."

Ida sketched.

"But not so tight that it makes my head hot or gives me a headache."

Ida erased.

"It won't catch on fire. I can wash it with my overalls when it gets dirty. And I can fold it up and carry it in my pocket if I don't want to wear it."

Ida finished sketching. "Open your eyes, Stormy. How about this?" Ida showed her drawing to Stormy.

Stormy stared at the picture. "It's perfect! This is the hat I want! This is the hat for a railroad man! Where can I buy one?"

"You can't," said Ida. "This hat doesn't exist. I made it up by drawing what you described. But now that I know what the hat looks like, I'm sure I can sew one for you."

"Would you do that for me?" Stormy asked. "I promise that from now on I'll listen to everything you have to say."

"It's a deal," said Ida.

Ida looked in the closet. She found one of Stormy's old baseball caps. She cut off the top and made a new one out of canvas. It looked like a bubble. Ida extended and re-covered the old brim and attached it to the new top.

"Try it on," she said to Stormy.

Stormy put the hat on his head. It fit just right. "It's exactly what I've been looking for!" he exclaimed, admiring himself in the mirror.

Stormy wore his hat to the railroad yard on Monday morning. He made the run to Chicago and back.

The hat didn't blow off.

It didn't get in his way.

It didn't catch fire.

It didn't give him a headache.

It got dirty, like his overalls. But it would wash clean again.

And when Stormy didn't need his hat, he tucked it away in his pocket. Ida had done it! She had created the best hat for a railroad man.

29

"Hey, Stormy! Where'd you get that hat? I want one, too," each of the trainmen said.

"You're out of luck, boys," said Stormy. "There's only one hat like this in the whole wide world, and it's mine. Ida made it for me."

"Would she make hats for us?"

"She might. Why don't you ask her?"

Engineers, brakemen, firemen—everyone who worked on the railroad wanted a hat like Stormy's. Orders came in from all over the country. There were too many hats for Ida to make by herself, so she and Stormy opened a factory. Soon they were sending hats to railroad men around the world.

More than a hundred years have passed since Ida made that hat for Stormy. Today, wherever you find trains, you'll find people wearing Stormy's hat. It's the only one that's right for a railroad man—and a railroad woman.

They owe it all to Ida, who knew exactly what Stormy needed.
And to Stormy, who listened to Ida.

Author's Note

George "Stormy" Kromer (1876–1970) was an engineer on the Chicago & North Western Railroad. He loved baseball as much as he loved trains. Stormy played on semiprofessional teams throughout the Midwest.

In Stormy's time, engineers and brakemen wore derbies or fedoras. Neither of those hats stayed on long in the high winds that blew through a locomotive cab. After losing his hat too many times, Stormy vowed to find one that would stay on his head and meet the needs of a trainman.

Stormy described his ideas to his wife, Ida, who was a talented seamstress. In the autumn of 1903, she took one of Stormy's baseball caps and made it into the hat that railroad workers have worn ever since.